THE PENGUIN POETS
THE VARIOUS LIGHT

Alfred Corn was born in Georgia in 1943. After earning his
B.A. and M.A. degrees in French literature at Emory and Co-
lumbia universities in 1965 and 1967, he taught at Columbia,
spent a year in Paris as a Fulbright Fellow, and then returned to
New York City to work as an editor at *University Review*. Ar-
ticles by him have appeared in *The New York Times, Parnassus,
Georgia Review,* and other periodicals, and his poetry has been
published in such publications as *The New Yorker, Saturday
Review, American Review, The Nation, Poetry,* and *Perspective.*
In 1974 he won *Poetry*'s George Dillon Memorial Prize, and in
1976 his first collection of poetry, *All Roads at Once,* was de-
scribed by James Merrill, amid critical acclaim, as "a new win-
dow onto the world" and "an extremely beautiful first book."
Harold Bloom said of Alfred Corn's second book, *A Call in the
Midst of the Crowd* (published by Penguin Books in 1978), "I
know of nothing else of such ambition and realized power in
Corn's own generation of American poets." Alfred Corn has
also taught at Yale University and Connecticut College. He
lives in New Haven, Connecticut.

THE VARIOUS LIGHT

ALFRED CORN

PENGUIN BOOKS

Penguin Books Ltd, Harmondsworth,
Middlesex, England
Penguin Books, 625 Madison Avenue,
New York, New York 10022, U.S.A.
Penguin Books Australia Ltd, Ringwood,
Victoria, Australia
Penguin Books Canada Limited, 2801 John Street,
Markham, Ontario, Canada L3R 1B4
Penguin Books (N.Z.) Ltd, 182–190 Wairau Road,
Auckland 10, New Zealand

First published in the United States of America in
simultaneous hardcover and paperback editions by
The Viking Press and Penguin Books 1980

LIBRARY OF CONGRESS CATALOGING IN PUBLICATION DATA
Corn, Alfred, 1943–
The various light.
I. Title.
PS3553. 0655V3   1980b   811'.54   80-17644
ISBN 0 14 042.284 6

Printed in the United States of America by
American Book–Stratford Press, Inc.,
Saddle Brook, New Jersey
Set in CRT Caslon

The author wishes to acknowledge a National Endowment for the Arts award for the year 1979–80, and to thank editors of the following publications, where poems, often in different form, first appeared:

Argo, "AELFRED MEC HEHT GEWYRCAN"
Canto, "Meridional," "Pantoum," "Two Places in New England"
Connecticut Artists, "November Leaves"
The Hudson Review, "The Outdoor Amphitheater"
The Kenyon Review, "At the Grave of Wallace Stevens," "*Lacrimae Rerum*"
The Nation, "Herb Garden," "Shores," "The Village"
The New Leader, "Reading *Pericles* in New London"
The New Republic, "The Beholder," "Terrier," "Town Center in December"
The New York Review of Books, "Maine Real Estate"
The New Yorker, "Grass"
Paris Review, "Interior," "One to One"
Partisan Review, "Gloze"
Poetry, "Audience," "Cornwall," "Prime Minister in Retirement," "Remembering Mykinai," "Repertory," "Tanagra"
Salmagundi, "A Bid," "Debates," "September Inscription"
Shenandoah, "Moving: New York–New Haven Line"
The Yale Review, "The Progress of Peace"

FOR J.D. McCLATCHY

CONTENTS

THE VARIOUS LIGHT

WELLS FARGO BANK
Transaction Record

Branch # 0633 10   Deposit

Account Number   Amount
0609272489 $111,146.30

Transaction # 021 0024
10:41am   08/12/99   Credited: 08/12/99

Why Rush To The Bank? Use Direct Deposit

Thank you, Yoon

199

$5 461 13

461 01

TERRIER

Yes, anybody's heart pounds when the world,
Benignly magisterial, turns round
And asks, "Whose dog are you? Let's hear you speak!"
If only tugs and growls could do the trick;
Leaping and barking, a fellow gets hoarse, called down,
Left panting in a heap of blank fatigue.
Still, the keenest sense instinctively *knows*.
(Through the lump in my throat I blurt this out
And hope it takes. Flashing a silver-nicked license,
I settle back with one ear pricked at Wait.)

And you, best friend, crouched at my feet in a rapture
Of animal attention bred on love,
Always fetch whatever ball I toss—
No inside task so golden as retrieval.
But who thinks the whole pack will come running
To play the fable's plucky role of sidekick?
The steady, loyal pet; a little spoiled,
Maybe, but nothing like a wolf. Here sport,
My lap! Put out your mitt, Old Man, and shake.
From eye to eye, another gust of soul.

I

MOVING:
NEW YORK–NEW HAVEN LINE

Taut on the leash, at last I have my way:
The train jolts off, just for a split-second
Immobilizing a porter I catch sight of
Through my window, pushing his cart. The platform's
A treadmill or a backward rack; for, his feet
Notwithstanding, he grinds into reverse,
Left behind in underground darkness. . . .
That forward-backward prank gets cruelly played
On every car or truck that races with us
Along the paralleling highway; try
As they might, our motion slowly brakes them,
It sends them backsliding faster and faster
Behind; a feeling I recall from nightmares
(Nightmares, and, to tell the truth, from "real life"
As well). Another stunt of overtaking
(Like my own sharp about-face two months back)
Is the fateful rotation a car makes:
Trunk to grill we see it, a slow, pivotal
Display—practiced, in fact, on every near
Item in the window, especially trees,
Their radially branching form flung into perfect
Umbrella turns (clockwise, because I see them
From the train's left side). Indian file they run
And pirouette together, the closest rank
So much quicker than others farther out,
Which fall behind at a desultory pace.

(This constant shuttle between two points has made
At least some aspects of the pattern clearer.)
Passengers riding backwards, though, see things
Otherwise—and must feel guilty about it;
When I turn and catch them looking, their eyes
Drop, and they assume a preoccupied
Air meant to mime some private train of thought.
Impatience? Funk? A half-wish for derailment?
(They don't have *you* waiting for them, smiling. . . .)
Our steady, legato impetus is barred
At regular intervals by metal poles
That fly by in a soon predictable
Tempo, echoed also by the sag and soar
Of highstrung staff lines hanging down between.
I keep looking for groups of eighth-note starlings
To give the gallop a tune, but none are there,
Nor ever even a rest, just a continuing
Inaudible rush, variably elastic
According to our speed, which hums the landscape
Into a final tableau of motion itself—
A thing so strangely still at its utmost—
The factories, ashheaps, stations, transports caught
In a fastness that wants to hold my eyes
In thrall and lock me up in sleepless dreams.
(Your voice is putting accents in the transit,
Pulling me toward you on a silken line—
*And dreams   that ran   on time   were Vehicles-
For-Something-Else. . . .?*)

*

My mind winks on again—yes, there's that river
We cross here now, the same and always different.
A breeze intangible to me suddenly
Wakes the trees and blows on the gray water,
Shriveling the surface into a kind of
Elephant skin. A chevron of migrant geese
Flies into it—bull's eye straight to the heart
Of twenty concentric spreading circles. Water,
Birds, trees, swerve: how is it possible
To be moved in so many ways at once?

*

Our conductor shouts the listened-for station.
Though I've kept to one spot, the place has changed.
That, along with the name, which, red letter by
Reverse red letter, rolls toward me. Our shared
News—and the rest is neither here nor there,
Is anywhere we both shelter, still moving
Toward deeper welcomes, reunions. This racing
Panic will stop, once it's reminded we are
The only place I really want to go.

7

AT THE GRAVE
OF WALLACE STEVENS

Cedar Hill Cemetery, 21 March, 1978

"We should die except for death." And even then
We do? The brightness of this early sun's
One light with that other day, five decades now,
When you cleared your throat and took to words again,
Tossing off your metaphysical hurts like
Speech impediments.

The back-and-forth of light and breath wants to,
By tmesis, free contracted hopes in all
Uninsurable things; and let them be
No cause for cause's sake or pieties,
The welling spring, dumb tears, far gone in earth's
Bright particulars.

This simple stone, its ashen pink incised
With simple lilies and your easy name—
And hers, the household tokens you exchanged—
Faces eastward, where Hartford's towers daydream.
A cedar and a budding willow cast
Shadows on the graves

And grass, the last patches of fluent snow
Withdrawing into mud and air; as if
To say, Poverty, be changed to Poetry:

Let the veil be torn away, the weather cleared
For a green metathesis where lucid leaves
Damask this new ground!

Philosopher of one or two ideas,
Touching no strings that hadn't been given—
And all the notions you had had had had
From the first the gaiety of stammered baubles,
As a way to say hiho to blank zero,
Shouting down the void.

These sturdy upright burgher bedsteads with light
And shadow sharply ruled in granite tell
Their legends to a sky *bleu ciel*—a thing
As it is in itself, but translated
Into distanced thought that comes nearer
Rhyming sound with mind;

And clouds freely associating one
Into another, still play to your own
High theater, tropical, boreal,
Informing and deforming what you saw
As final mercy, but, for other eyes,
Less than final loss.

To draw a golden bead on the marginal. . . .
Can you be felt as patient with a bitter
Restorative, a lighter régime building
Ruins to replace what was not at first
Meant for ruin? (Ask, as though you stood in this
Place of numbered stones—

Which might be graves of ancestors in that
Low country of the mind, at the middle height
Of dark, warring with nature's war, Antares
Pendant on the night, the noted vireo
And corydalis weeping over the cold
Spurls of passing time. . . .)

The bluster, the tawny lions of other
Marches take their place in gentle order.
To feel the flaw as a widening melt
And hear the wind speaking along bright strings—
The sun's a hat to be put on and then
Lightly doffed to you.

If it's still right to "like words that sound wrong,"
Take these to sleep on where you rest, under blue
Featherweight shadows, your tireless vigil now
The highway's self-renewing whisper, far
And near: endlessly it keeps revolving what
Time has written down.

THE VILLAGE

for James Merrill

Green tunnel through maples;
A bridge over twinned pairs of rails
    Shunts the car right to the square.
Houses, high fence, where trumpet vines
    Downspilling in jubilee

Herald today's parade:
Our Lady of Fatima, reverenced
    Here in Azores Portuguese.
A white church looks on; the sunstruck
    Brasses glitter and are gold.

Natural life wants form:
In their clipped garden two women
    Smoke, review without surprise
The candidly outsize lilies,
    Think back on Europe between

Two wars; they have discarded
The city (safe in quarantine
    Down at the newsstand two streets
Over.) The milky, byword fog
    Blows in, punctuated now

And then by dim C-sharps
Out past the breakwater, the gamut
    Changeless as that half-ellipse

11

Fanlight cut under the gables
  Of every Federal house

On Main or Water Street.
A summer visitor is lost
  In the evening's gray dissolves
Among the blistered, drydock hulls
  Of the indistinct boatyard.

He walks and takes his time
From the tempo of a harbor
  Told by the metronome masts
Of sailboats made to balance at
  Andante ma non troppo.

Old pilings—each crowned with
A comedic gull tiny whims set
  Guffawing, head thrown back, maw
Wide and human—cannot translate
  The water's calligraphic

Renderings of what they are:
But a mind at the very end
  Of the pier identifies
With those mercurial gerunds,
  Trembling, reflecting, darkening. . . .

He will blink at weathered
Boards, the sumptuous disrepair
  Of his nautical surround,

12

Where covered docks sag and moult, board
    Wears down to a moiré grain

As gray as fog or thought;
Pass the gaspumps' stiff attention,
    The chest marked ICE with ice-capped
Capitals; and, like an old board
    Himself, play softly down his kind,

A passage on wooden keys
Toward his interim house, the stardeck
    Night will canopy with clear skies,
Galaxies, the bright dust of space—
    At the last a near, distinguished thing.

NOVEMBER LEAVES

Morning finds them silver, quite a killing
At the trees' expense. And, like the delicate milling
That seconds the die-cut dial of a dime,
The cold has etched each margin with shining rime.

Small change—but enough for what there is to buy:
Those white-sale blankets, woolens of the snows
Winter tosses down from its vault of sky.
Green copper silver time grows on trees; and goes.

TOWN CENTER IN DECEMBER

They stand as though standing's what they came for.
Some deep conviction keeps them shivering
In their boots, ungloved hands pocketed, elbows
Clenched to the ribs, the whole effect much like
A bellows; which huffs and puffs out cold plumes
Of whitened breath, the little of it used
For speech doled out unwillingly. Words find
Their feet here only in a systole-
Diastole that telegraphs remorse and fear,
Cash sums galvanic to the homemade iamb:
I'm eighty dollars overspent so far;
I've really got to try and hold it down.
But how get past the ordered zeal that laid
This trap of civic grids, where pigeons, urban
If not yet tame, beetle like us across
A green decked out with colored lights, thousands,
(To help us like the weight of extra bags
And run through the midday hours pushing in
And out of revolving doors, steal after steal,
Held up by the bargains there)? We go, we stop,
We crane upward at smokeglare skies and hope
To see a sign—if only handed down
From the billboard's impassive, ad hoc person.
The puzzle in his face is reassuring;
He seems to know that we've been treading water
And no doubt wants to help. . . . You opposite,
Chock-a-block ranks, wait; and stare us down.

(Familiar inmates of so many lines,
We gathered here to be alone, did we?)
The bus glides up and stops; gusts, lurches,
Erasing all your glasses, coats and notions
As broadcast chimes begin to strike the time.
They run ahead of you all the way home,
A place never very far from here,
Nor from a bar less thirst than doggedness
Will draw some unresigned ones to around ten.
What brighter festivities would you ask for?
Let lights light up, glow on glow with the glasses
Night after night of whiskey, beer and gin!
Until the New Year drops you off again,
The post you think of as your own, where you
Will stand and wait, cold and numb with waiting.

INTERIOR

So many verticals, and
How every object is a bar
To thought, the table
Not cleared away.

An emptied wineglass
White windows reflect in
Billowing like sails.
Plate of the finished meal—

Knife: salt; the seated body
Opposite suddenly adding up
To two glass eyes
In as many dimensions, depth

Just a change from large to small.
Afternoon begins indirectly
With brine burns of light
From behind. Nothing can stop it.

TWO PLACES IN NEW ENGLAND

i

Out on the speechless white plain
The snowshoes shush no sound unless their own.
Blue with no ice-clouds silent on high,
Aeronautic blue clear to the pole;
And a polar bloom infuses the fields.

Dry and watered grist, bear the weight.
Keep the record of each cross-hatched step.

A dozen half hoops,
The barbed raspberry canes
Anchored in snow, a wicker the dustiest
Brown rose.
No waxwing or winter wren nimbly stationed
On the stubble's threaded glaze; or on
The thick brakes of underbrush at field edge.
Strawy nearer weeds stand stoic
Over the snow, beside fallen bright berries,
Blooddrops in beaded spoor:
Some dainty velvet pelt, brown by black chevron,
Taken by a hawk, by an ermined owl,
Scripture on wing.

The bare beech, carven and muscular:
At each meeting of limbs a crater
Filled with snow, grails of light.

Will it always be damson bristle on the hills,
The trees and brush galena-bright in sun,
With jaggedly branched white birches singled out
Among them, frozen lightning-bolts
Shot from the ecliptic's great crossbow?

Winter, know, be, and say more than this
Intricate featureless plain of ice,
Shadowed by hemlock,
The needles' tight black plan,
Weeds their own monument,
Seeds their shorthand,
And, on snowslope façades up the rocks,
Scatterings of tiny scythes,
The split beech husks, twisted
Apart, opened, emptied, made past.
Winter, timeless machine, cold presence of the past—
A cold that is polar and blue, in the pastures and snowfields.

ii

The fresh-rinsed rural chrysalis breaks open—
A wing, two wings, trying their fitness to the wind.
The air develops, but not stirs the gravestone,
A motto's Doric, sampler truth,
The marble vigil of a willow standing downcast,
Even in New England, above an antique urn.

Yet we only look and pass.
That a willow would be yellow

All in cascade over the brook
Where wobbling hoses and vocal jellies murmur,
Water; or bluegreen swords have risen,
Equinox germinator, from corms under mud;
And I take this sighting of you
In lost profile against the field—
It comes down to water, and things best made.

Water brought them, the builders and rebuilders—
Threshold to rooftree, shingle or clapboard.
"Trouble to build and rebuild the spring!"
Says the durable warbler coming back:
More subtle homespuns for a nobler nest,
Glovelike, to cradle the fragile prospects in.
Tireless burden of returning
Travelers, skill renewed on veteran wings:
Like a molding made of sound and motion,
Egg-and-dart, egg-and-dart, frames the air.

Naïve catkins, pollen-dusted;
Gold of an hour stayed in stacks of forsythia.
Light, be laid like malleable leaf
On polished branches, heraldic buds.

Side by side, across the springy compost,
We find the path again;
Past a broken toadstool circle,
Ghost meats and umber gills, a scattered henge.
Jack-in-the-pulpit back in the shadows
Of a cedar grove is holding forth to show the way—

And what crisper gesture now, spathe and spadix,
Than your green- and white-ribbed flourish?

Here: a rocky seat beside the flood.
At tips of leaves let beads of water-glass
Gather in the terrestrial sphere.
If rivers keep their history,
They keep it silent, all the liquid knowledge
Reworded in one kindly play—
Light on the water, on trees—a face—
To be so chancy, a burden so great—
Letting some things go—that others come—
Taking and giving speech away—the various light.

Unwrap the message hidden in a wound
Or a word: a branching spray of avowals, cut,
Massed, left to glide deathward in a vase. . . .
Face to face, a match, together until we choose;
And afterwards as well, isn't too much to hope for.
Still no sign of the chance to balance off
Independence and devotion—the armature jangled,
Door- and telephone-bell, errand, project,
A wave hello-goodby on the fraying wing.
Unmeasurable, the drag of countered origins,
The wind-chill factor, circumstantial walls.
There's always been a question, too,
Of satire mixed in with the mortar
Of our homemade, honeyed, subfusc nougat.
Faithful in your detachment, clear-eyed, marooned;
This you reserve to me—the person in the round,
A dark, and then the light side of the earth,
Warmth that spreads at a touch, as at dawn;
The play, the heft and pungency. Prized.
Best, I think, to leave chiaroscuro alone.
(And classify your cub or mooncalf name
Along with much else so sacredly banal
It has to take the reasonable vow of silence.)
A fresh effort sends me prospecting for clues,
Browsing in your empty study, paneled
With research and labor, leather, faded gold,
Patriarchal tobacco. Lamplight does and doesn't

Sum up a mind's household. Nor are you among those
Most at ease when being photographed or described.
In no uncertain terms, spleen, tinder,
Everready rejoinder when a mood strikes,
Head in flames, the shaft breaking smartly in two.
Your turn or mine to lay it out again,
How the all-intent have trouble conceding even
The clearest-cut foul, the pang's too sharp? Who,
When the smoke clears this time, will be missing
In action? One half, contracted to an unavoidable sky.
By magic you come back, gleam and scattered debris;
Pencil in hand, the cigarette sketching gestures
As gauze floats upward, unfurled, as the sun
Goes down. Free of one more day; and how much striving.
Remains the tireless need to be reimaged,
Where we were, where we are, the wide-ranging seesaw
Of the team, in full array, a full-blooded portrait.
(What questions don't dissolve in a green-brown gaze.)
Focus: the doorframe opposite, by three-quarter light,
Aplomb poised on the balls of your feet, the elbows
You nurse, and—just this once—the gravest of smiles.
The album fills, it grows substantial;
Superseded, replaced, updated, changed—
The candid, casual arrangements made.

II

OXYGEN

Routine and daily, black-and-white—
The newsprint kindling scorched and smoked.
In airless rooms, no catching on:
The firebrand *Phoenix* would have choked.

Say hazard and the fuel were one:
Transforming fire, still want your turn?
Then you must have, to enact your rite,
A chance to breathe, and freedom to burn.

LACRIMAE RERUM

No closer than that; then some will prefer
The middle distances, a touch farther
Off from fact; if only to discover

Perspectives where such a limited thing
Multiplies into so much of everything.
Did you always want to be surveying

Rainbows, anemones, glisterings, veined
Marbles? No, and wouldn't have invented
This labyrinth of noises, clanged, whispered,

And hummed. It makes for a Gulliver's passion,
The million threads of perception—
That, plus another drawback, the sincere fustian,

Old fears that seldom seem altogether
Real and yet still operate. The wider
Net of words matters more than the speaker;

And if reason trumpets the nearing collapse
Of reason—that might be just one more trap.
(This has done duty as the three loud raps.)

     *

At first no one assumes it's purposeful.
Each separate form, each color draws you
Further into the plot. Told you're obliged

28

To assemble it, you smile and sidestep,
Frown and back off; but a huge hand nudges you
Away from the sidelines. The animal roar,

And now a black curtain of engulfment,
Temperatures, the surge of speed and night,
And sound dropping out just before that blind

Slalom, without the ghost of an idea—
But there it is: the islanded city,
Fair, populous, all inviting windows.

Unprompted, the streets rise up, a slow flood
Of dream, abstract, ionized, asking us
To come in out of the light, stop and rest.

Any spot is conspiratorial,
Claustral, the unkempt setting we stand in
Bright contrast to. Someone has seen it all.

                    *

The story had me change trains where a winged man
Smiled down, who flew by smiles alone, pinions
Just a plumage—the insignia of flight.

First, a dim rendezvous among the rocks:
Comprehensiveness was their promise, one
Hand-held globe, small and mine. "Here's your seat."

A little glass orchestra begins to play,
Each violin washed in platinum and strung
With silver wires. Silicon flutes, pianos

That speak when struck in quartz-crystal shatters,
The harps spewing icy fountains of soda,
Virtuosic, ebullient, vitreous.

The first violin, polished to a snap,
Ripples bright mercuries. Owl-eyed, I peer
Into twin incised *f*-holes: nothing there.

Oh. A small bright point is growing, widening.
A tiny Acropolis, cast in metal:
Temples of Mirth, Ironic Capitals. . . .

                *

There's an object-lesson in our gestures,
The secrets told, foolish offense-taking. . . .
Points that nowise prevented one bland, partial

Morning from bringing me the news—awake,
True, but unprepared. Simply that it was
Given: a blank headache. And had come to stay.

Not that hopes for a dry accommodation
Should be dropped. Pain, you can't keep on spinning
That way forever; much prolonged, you become

Just a character, the sign of what never
Changes. I wonder whether the others, those
Not shown how it might be understood as sport

(Although one at fantastic stakes), sometimes
Feel the rooted chill of their own fixity.
Do they try answering to a dangled

Choice not really one, are they also left
Unprovided? I shouted to them, waved banners,
Sent up flares: little firecrackers of applause.

                    *

(Recognition as realization:
Blinded with eyes, youth sees only surface—
Tears, the spirit-lamp, put out of focus;

But once the questions tried have failed, the old
Don fulminates against them: the pasture
Is a sea; be the island it defends,

No longer wandering the length of that
Peninsula, arid, darkly castled,
Where none but a king is truly *real.*

Or so I read the myth; and took as mine
One more unseasonable obligation,
Laid in clear amber, a new anthemion:

Each pause, each breath or heartbeat was concern
Pleading so unlawful a reflection,
Caught in the blade of the sickle I held,

Would be turned against me, meant to be struck down,
Lying alone under midnight, the sky peerless
With grist of phosphor, my starred caparison.)

*

Yet who'd have time to think purposefully,
Confronted with that violet or even
Madder-colored choosing? Which may finally

Be why I'm there, to assay whatever
Sensation tried to leave as residue;
And effectively white out the distracting

Features, send them through a private "dolby."
Undaunted still, the hindsight saga keeps
Imploding, crab nebulae suddenly

Played at fast-backward and with a pounding
Like surf inside that echo-cave of bone.
Look for flowering vines, Heavenly Blues,

A walk under an alley of lindens,
Near anaesthesia with the powdery scent,
Lachrymal sunlight, green dark, light, dark, light. . . .

*

A fury, miniaturized, envenomed,
Stung me into action or at least spleen—
One step away from that precise ambient,
Those few, star-pale days. Opposed coinfaces;
A deep relation told. I'd call it bitter
If what the bees took from it didn't keep.

REMEMBERING MYKINAI

Guides urged us, praised us up to the Lion Gate, its
Carved lintel "brought from twenty or possibly
  Two hundred miles away" and wedged in
  Place by the gods or a tyrant's hybris.

High up, the fallen muscular citadel,
Great blocks the winds had modeled and smoothed like the
  Hard flesh of some remembered Argive—
  Vengeful Orestes, the seed of Pelops?

Nearby, the beehive tomb lay, an underground
Dome sunk in gloom. Its resonance chilled us, as
  Trapped flies, whose droning stunned the eardrum,
  Sluggishly spiraled above our comments.

Stones, stone, the life they hewed; and the self a dark
Construct, both tomb and citadel. Why will a
  Dead hour, when change breeds mishap, rise to
  Strike us, metallic and harsh as noonday?

Rocks, thyme, the wind-scorched Peloponnese—to which
Years stretch in mute kilometers back. But those
  Strong measures taken, steps our feet took,
  Echo through ruins like yours, Mykinai.

TANAGRA

Hellenic times so slight as you a ware
Foreknew how it was that laws like gravity's
Had immersed your stance in streamlike drapery
And fixed your earthen gaze on Theban stars.
Since you were cast to see as sculpture sees,
Change you cannot support you will ignore,
Memento of future but still classic terrors,
The darkening pull down perpetuity.
That myth invoked, assume it as one more
Mantle. Too near to breath to choose the dead,
You help the traveler ford the dream he dreads,
Who stand in fluted robes on modern shores,
A single column, capital your head
That bears the pondered weight of what we are.

AELFRED MEC HEHT GEWYRCAN

Motto on the Alfred Jewel, Ashmolean Museum

Under rock quartz, cloisonné:
Green of a chrysoprase, the blue of lapis;
And the whole encased in gold.
In intricate gold, the scaly dragon's head—
Earless, blunt-muzzled, staring—
Guarding the king's portrait, and belling, in Saxon,
"Alfred had me be fashioned."

Ruler in Wessex, the king plucked back London
From the Danes; they had been the scourge
Visited on a flock gone astray—its error,
It could not read. The king read
Denmark back into the sea: Boethius,
Augustine's *Soliloquies,*
The *Cura Pastoralis,* in a new tongue.

As justice is a jewel
Alfred ordered the just kingdom: from Northmen
Free, this green province walled round
By blue, its shepherd the scepter and golden
Word—to which he returned then,
"That in the midst of earthly ills he sometimes
Might think of heavenly things."

PRIME MINISTER IN RETIREMENT

Is, and has been raining several days.
Dull as rain, our plates of tarnished pewter
Line the walls. The tea—and fine Earl Grey's—
Has cooled inside her cup; it doesn't suit her.

Past, present, they boil down to much the same,
Don't they? Yesterday (and every) we read.
I'd say the future made less sound a claim:
Bonds are promised gold, not gold; and "lead"

In print's no more than scrip until a voice
Or context has determined whether it
Commands or means base metal. Speech is choice—
Home rule. I've made mine and weather it.

CORNWALL

Sun rising at your back,
Cross the dry bed of the Tamar;
Wheels whisking the road behind
Unroll the land like carpet.

No poet, Cornwall?
None to praise the velvet pastures
With hand-hewn cows, couchant
Among purslane, granite and sorrel;

The faraway hillside meadow where
Sheep no bigger than rice grains graze,
Feeding, feeding like aphids
By the blasted pine and stunted oak?

St. Piran, patron of miners,
Come down in the shape of a sea-gull,
Crucified on your trim white wings,
Your halo bright as the top of a tin!

Bless the wolfram dug for treasure
At Castle-an-Dinas, heaped up there
Beside the brick stacks belching forth
Smoke-gouts, a wreath to heaven.

And do you take away the pagan stain
From the dolmens of Mufra and Chun,

The monoliths in the parish
Of charitable St. Buryans?

Best loved of his grandsire Alfred,
AEthelstan took this for England,
He tried to: lengthy Anglo-Saxon
Wrangles in the witenagemot.

"By Pol, Tre and Pen,
You may know the Cornish men."
But not one now will crawl nine times
Against the sun and through a stone

Ring, to be cured of rickets;
And today a boy was broken, died—
Stealing eggs from sea-gull nests,
He fell on the rocks at Falmouth.

And another struck by a black bolt
Flung down through high-tension lines—
Green glass fixtures afire with sun
Climbed recklessly among.

The spiked hawthorns all remember,
Some flushed pink as though with wine,
Blent with the high, savage hedgerows
That cicatrize the fields.

Remember, too, the sturdy inns,
Each with its peruke of thatch—

Trelawney, The Pillars, The Badger,
Smugglers, Three Pilchards, The Sloop—

And the sea-mists that lost to view
One lighthouse in St. Ives Bay.
The holiday-makers paced and paced,
And stared uncomprehendingly

At outdoor trays of turbot, cod,
Conger, dogfish, ray and skate.
(Cornish wrestlers at Agincourt:
And this is the English Riviera.)

Sun declining, but there's still time
To push down to the toe of the county,
Tipping into the Atlantic, O
The cliffs and sea-pinks at Land's End!

No magic if by a trick of light
And cross-hatched waves, the souls
Of the drowned move on the water,
Film-like now in purple shrouds.

They pace, call out, flail their arms
Backward into the deep; and they surely
Have telegrams for long-erased names
Who didn't drown, though will have died.

One changing-color silhouette
Has guessed the shores you left behind;

And knows the course, the sun-road down,
One last anchor in Dingle Bay;
Then out to the edge of the world:
Here There Be Monsters, and your home.

MAINE REAL ESTATE

Is hardship renewal? The cold waves
Keep coming in, little restrained
By islands offshore, where they ride
Ringed around by small, stripped-down craft.

Every lookout gazes seaward;
A whole township ignoring the signs
Nailed to walls and porches—a sale,
A July sale on houses. Mist

Rises from the lawns, stalling in the elms;
Shingle slumps, white paint scales, as though
Some genie steamed up from his oil-lamp
Had waved a fist and shouted, Collapse!

Dockside the Maritime Academy's
Grandest classroom sits at anchor,
Drawing a cadet up the gangplank,
His face deadpan, like the face

Of the infantryman a century
At ease on the green, forward inclined,
Granite rifle by his side.
No attention paid. Each citizen

Is visibly minding his business
Even when, reflexively, he

Barks out an "Afternoon"
To others on foot, who nod and pass.

What high, stinging whine gives it away—
That all, the most skeptical,
The most assured, are expecting news?
Word may come with the fog; cocooned

In a morning paper; or brought by the stranger:
Something else that must be borne. . . .
Briny droplets tingle in suspension;
The screen door of the general store

Reliably slams behind the postman,
Who stops, squints, tips back his cap
To catch, where it has broken through,
The pallor of the northern sun.

READING *PERICLES* IN NEW LONDON

The driven are the only ones to read
In cars; and double that for a patched-up thing
Like *The Prince of Tyre*. We've rolled to a standstill here,
A town that knew at least this much about us:
We'd need some classic service station, like Gulf
Or Mobil Oil . . . whose tricolor properties
These are: signs, pumps, uniforms,
All red-white-and-blue. (No stars or stripes, though.)
Throttles gun up and down; my nose crinkles
At the vibrant stench of fuel tainting the air;
And billboards across the way are advertising—
The Mystic Marina! (Jokes, coincidence,
And anachronism, the stuff of dreams and plays. . . .)
This Prologue says, "The older a good thing, the better."
Which doesn't quite account for classics, texts
A few dedicated bookworms devour,
Otherwise enshrined in gilt-edged neglect.
What makes me keep on turning pages and not
Just grunt, The End—I mean, since protest nudges
And says, Don't miss the goings-on around you.
Might be stubbornness; as well as glimmers
That I, not Shakespeare's play, am being judged.
(It would be different if we called to witness
His finest plays—*The Tempest, Hamlet, Lear*—
Which do, we feel, still sound contemporary
Depths.) I wonder what the Soul of the Age
Would make of New London. Would he think our brash,

If aging new world, El Dorado on wheels,
Stood on a plane with the old, a proper stage
For acts of global import framed in speech?
Well, everywhere you turn there are "characters";
And snatches of salty talk, some with a faint
Shakespearean ring—like this man's here, who grins
And takes a credit card as sunlight gilds
His hands. The chance for high-octane lines
Is to fuel many vehicles, deluxe
And budget compact both. Stately psalms,
You couldn't know you'd end up here as proverbs,
Of the party with drabs and scrapes of times
You never dreamed. . . . Indeed the truest author
Will put little credit in a captive future,
Betraying his age by having none, and all
Of them at once. Now first, now second, now
Third—a different gear for every scene,
Up to the last. Mystic Marina, be
Our oracle. The dolphin sometimes swims
In oil-stained seas; is it less delphic then?

GRASS

At this range, it's really monumental—
Tall spears and tilted spears, most
Blunted by the last mowing.
A few cloverleafs (leaves?)
And infant plantains fight
For their little plot of ground.
Wing-nuts or boomerangs, the maple seeds
Try to and really can't take root.
There's always more going on
Than anyone has the wit to notice:
Look at those black ants, huge,
In their glistening exoskeletons.
Algebraically efficient,
They're dismembering a dragonfly—
Goggle-eyed at being dead
And having its blue-plated chassis,
Its isinglass delicately
Leaded wings put in pieces.
When you get right down to it,
The earth's a jungle.
The tough grass grows over and around it all,
A billion green blades, each one
Sharply creased down the spine.
Now that I've gotten up to go,
It's nothing but a green background
With a body-shaped dent left behind.
As the grass stretches and rises,
That will go, too.

SEPTEMBER INSCRIPTION

R.T.S.L. 1917–1977

We saw the sky descending, gray and white,
And idling oil-black limousines receive
Their passengers, air charged with held-off rain,
The still resisted fall of things that leave.
Studied gaze, to you it would be plain;
But you have taken flight,
Your remnant meaning bared and left to lead
From now a second kind of life. Our own
Persists under noonday clouds where loss is shown
How final words must come to spell as deed.

REPERTORY

You feel odd seeing libido staged
In a theater once a church;
For lobby, this vestibule—acrid,
Packed, and loud, a remission of sense
Between the first and final acts.
Let it go that no one bothers now
To make or damn or save appearances.
Whatever is not unredeemed
Must manifestly be redeemed.
Evenings like this one almost tempt you
To face the republic and the music,
Intransitive as the verb "to be,"
Your scruples imprecise or just not
Present, betting on an erotic plum
Time and expertise wither into
Another agent of comic relief.

Witnessed fiction fuses the parterre
Into a single man, each acted pause,
Word, or gesture featly shared by all:
That rapt gaze was truly spectacular.
Now step outside into the friendly cold,
Remembering what common sense destroys.
And if you put the issues intensely
Your homely mind may flare up and disperse
A myriad pointblank stars. Even
The hunchbacked moon may stumble, unbalanced
As anyone who strives or has no peer.
"God, the true classic, is a little obscure."

THE PROGRESS OF PEACE

I.

THE SEASONS

Unearthly, and only of earth,
They were born with the eastern spring,
Dawn startling off prismatic dews;
Flown south in summer, to turn back
With a cool westering autumn
And peak with the northern winter,
Clockwise around the compass rose:
Who winds the sundial, heaven knows.

II.

FIVE SENSES

For if thoughts will always be racing clouds
The dull, the hidebound can't choose to follow,
Now that noon's the flagship on ground-swell fields,
Milkweeds in flower, each with a monarch
Pinned to it, divine right of laziness,
The disbelieving suspension of will,
Prone, supine—it's no way to deliver
The gods, themselves underachievers, but
Who shed for this day (as though we were kings)
Distilled light like a spirit glaze on things.

III.

SOLOMON'S SEAL

Then number as many lapses as you can name
(You be the jury provided all of you're quick
At riddles and will bargain as you did at six,
When grammar came in like blue afternoons and books
Began to speak, persuading you to other soils
And suns, those lights a hidden spark answered well to,
The pearl of price hardened and lustrous around pain,
As though it promised some afterworld dialogue with
Those who *knew*); constellate thought, Chinese checkerboard,
Its patterned holes like a colander's, the leaps
Short legs take through forms, distinguishing sense from noise,
Ripeness understood as mostly a tone of voice.

IV.

THE PLEIADES

These questions turn inward on themselves and may still call back
Accents of warmth and spaciousness: halcyon envoy, begin,
Leave your cut-out silhouette in the fiery tapestry,
Shadow-puppet of the void, the midnight summons, a mask
In retreat approaching us, far from the universal
Hub its speed vies with and cancels, a memory of sails
To propel it before high winds that never rose and so
Can never fail, but stay going—as in the realm of fact,
Where all a lens must do is make knowledge precipitate,
What we loved, were near and coming closer to, like athletes who
Took heart once they surmised those tiny figures, black on white,

49

Skating endless 8's, ice-fishing, or standing quietly
Under moss-grown eaves hung with tears and swords
    were what the race
Is run for, all the distance covered deeply found in place.

✽ ✽ ✽ ✽ ✽

III

A BID

By nature I dislike early successes.
So will you: the first steps to the happiest
Places don't feel golden or congenial.
I warn I promise nothing less than too much
Affective overdrive; steady to-and-fros
Between satisfaction and disappointment;
And premature aging. No question I have
My own doubts about the script, as it involves
Periodic disasters, vertigos, and
Pratfalls: aloft in a traveling balloon,
Feel those spinal thrills as hot-air hopes begin
To cool! And you'll also have to watch out for
Those around wearing blinders, whose stratagems
Will startle you: professed scruples of a high
Order; in practice, none, or one set displaced
By timely others justified as deeper.
Then, the touching belief in self-manufacture—
Millions on the rugged slopes of Mount Unique!
Each armed with a multiply useful pick-axe.
My place, you'll say, to suggest other models. . . .
If certain moonstruck nights suddenly a tree
Answers to the winds by having all its leaves
Turn coinlike silver with a quick glissando
Up the same shimmering scale, reflexively
Harmonized as a school of herring . . . well, that
Kind of choreography's too difficult,
Granted; but why not some form of mutual—?

No, you will always be testing the water
With each other; at the same time trying to
Avoid, if humanly possible, lengthy
Circumlocutions. All of you want to make
Different cases; though the one case by rights
Being made is—my own. But *you* talk. Still
Not convinced? Yet you must know the choice isn't
In fact yours. Looking into for example
The rear-view mirror, you see a little mask
With two holes for eyes, in foreground against
A forward-rushing landscape of rocks and leaves.
You see that; and you know I can use it. Come.

GLOZE

Life breaks its contracts and bargains with death.
Is it what we expected? Out as in,
Up, down—a seesaw of thought to season

Part of the pain, winter turning autumn,
The soldier rising from his grave? Light falls
On the man, but he does not become it.

A man who walked three days and nights never
Assumed that august personage was less
Imposing for his deeds of separation.

This calling for pomp, this parading death
Is no absolute; and we live without
A hope of memorial, as though days

In future time, a season of banished
Desire, when the wind sings and never stops,
Or when the blue wind stops and goes over

To the despair of means, will fade into
Voiceless heavens. The clouds remain and go
Under the dark. Nevertheless, in us
Their direction finds a ghostly echo.

DEBATES

A corded rope loops them around the waist.
They taste, they are wound and dream together
And apart: the figure would be dancing.

Weeks of study prepared these debates.
The marks of stress appeared, and deepened.
Bands of tensile color stretched
From forehead to bright forehead—breathless
Metamorphoses in contracted rooms, the near
Hopelessness of those about to respond:
As odious to shout yes as no.

A faceless window lights them here,
It has the rawness of a hole in space;
And the large, acute morning takes
One shot of them and another, the series
Peeled off and peeled off their bodies—
(Best played not too thin-skinned).
Practiced, they move through holds and locks,
Mariners at the helm of a clenched half-smile;
The kindness that wrenches, a vibrant wire
To get them across, regard laid aside,
Averted as a prowling beast is remembered,
The spool that winds up their minds being
Now one, now two. They go and come
Again and remain; are made ether,
Consumed, nourished, emptied, purified.

If the spectrum could lose all color now
And still be known by sight, these two have won,
Against the rope and the window, the light.

SONGS FOR FIVE
COMPANIONABLE SINGERS

I.
MERIDIONAL

A new way to imagine what love might be—
The women standing before their houses.
And I am high up in a dark-beamed room.

The women wear black, but not to mourn me.
White houses, geraniums, simple thresholds—
That is how they imagine love should be.

The antitwilight or the early moon
Lights a marble head slumped among vine-leaves,
Its blank eyes aimed at my dark-windowed room;

While to leaves and green spirals arachne
Secures her threads and draws them harp-string tight.
It's the way you imagine love to be

That tells your fortune—an inspiriting doom.
(The hidden flutist plays it tunefully
For someone high up in a dark-beamed room.)

Is blindness what I hear, or what I see?
The round tones float up like silver balloons.
One more way to imagine what love might be;
And I am high up in a dark-beamed room.

II.
THE BEHOLDER

Deep lake, surfaced sky that a drop disrupts,
The beholder is one not wooed by stages.
Will he look for light in your flawed water?

Ideals nurtured in a far other air
Summon him to your persuasive body,
Deep lake, surfaced sky that a drop disrupts.

Narcissus became his own pastoral,
The beholder's eye, a reflective beauty.
Did he look for light in your flawed water?

A beholding that is proof against all
Disproof—won't he prefer it to any
Deep lake, surfaced sky that a drop disrupts?

Echo's voice was just a trompe-l'oreille,
His own, sent back from where he never was.
Would he look for light in that flawed mimicry?

His sun rises on a new-found pleasure.
Deep lake, surfaced self that no drop disrupts,
An inward eye mirrors the purest blue.
He looks for light in his own clear water.

III.
AUDIENCE

Electric arcs describe your mind,
Casual as it wants to be.
Your sweeping periods toll with light
And draw your subjects through a maze:
Their power flows from this small cell.

It's more a throne-room than a cell,
You say. The bars put you in mind
Of music's polyphonic maze—
Though time, the signature you'd be
Void without, is measured here by light.

Melody's insubstantial   light
As air   each note a honeyed cell
Golden wholes   O harmonic bee
In tune with that collective mind
Dance directing as through a maze

To fragrant rooms evolved to amaze
With walls finely built   for delight
Is intricate no less than mind
Like flowers construed cell by cell
Music plays us as we want to be

A program that's too rich, maybe,
For every day—but there was a maze
Once, in England. . . . Trapped in a cell

Of privet; and my head went light;
Knew it was sunstroke but didn't mind. . . .

Beamed through a maze of cells the mind
Weighs just more than light   let it be

IV.
PANTOUM

"For Lucretius the sum of Be was Am."

Can they ever come back again,
The late architects of this room?
Am I the clock I say I am
For the day-star climbing toward noon?

The late architects of this room
Rose, instilled with proportioned dream.
For the day-star climbing toward noon
Their gold meanings were the golden mean.

Rose, instilled with proportioned dream,
Whatever flowers will fall in time.
Their gold meanings were the golden mean
To draughtsmen of a well-drawn line.

Whatever flowers will fall in time—
Memphis, Babylon, Athens, Rome.
To draughtsmen of a well-drawn line
Capitals define a mood in stone.

Memphis, Babylon, Athens, Rome—
They can never come back again.
Capitals define a mood in stone.
Am I the clock? I say I am.

V.
SHORES

The sun makes a seasonable return.
It photographs the breakers, it captures
What I was and am. I alone here, silent,

Ask this beach to change change into memoir—
Speechless at first, an illuminant that like
The sun makes a seasonable return.

These seeded grasses, stirred by a distant
Earthquake, nod indicative heads to call back
What I was. And am I alone here? Silent

And buried, that earthquake trembles inside me.
Each single stem of grass takes its measure from
The sun and makes a seasonable return.

A stem flexes between root and seed.
I feel the elation, the torsion between
What I was and am. I, alone here, silent,

Acknowledge the debt fruition will pay.
The sun makes a seasonable return,
And breath returns. The white waves are breaking
What I was. And I am alone here, speaking.

THE OUTDOOR AMPHITHEATER

Those first scenes, lapidary, paintbox bright:
The climb down, half circle
By concentric half circle, opening
On to wherever the beginning is—.
The mists lift, run before the sun,
Retreat, and shrink into the trees.
Now, it's the public park;
And I am standing by myself, inside
The amphitheater.
Picture a grassy stage on a low rise, opposite some
Old wooden bleachers stained leaf-green—
But when I begin to see them
(Somewhere between ages six and fourteen),
Already weathered to a pale olive.
'52? '53? Memory's hide-and-seek.
Around then, the days you saw little girls
Dressed like dolls—hairribbons, pinafores trimmed
In rose-red rickrack—and boys wearing navy shorts
Held up by suspenders, in warm weather
(Which came early that far south), Easters or
Summer afternoons, when people, whole families,
Their friends and distant relatives,
Went to the outdoor amphitheater.

The idea hard to get in focus is not how things
Looked but how the look felt, then—and then, now.
That grassy cradle had the appeal, first,

Of its agreeable siting and landscaping:
A fresh green plot enclosed by ranks of trees;
Sometimes a few clouds floating overhead
(Compare with the vague "idea" mentioned above).
Oyster-gray clouds, April week-ends;
But then, almost always the ceiling broke
Up into sunlight later in the day—
A fine-screened, copper-gold afternoon sun,
Which stayed bright till nearly everybody
Had gone home, leaving the picnic debris,
All the plates and cups—paper but surprisingly
Functional—the ice-cream sticks and mimeo programs. This
Then had to be collected and carted away
By an old man who used a—did it have a name?
A sort of stabbing stick; a stabber. He never attacked
The litter with much enthusiasm
Or worked longer than, if that, half an hour.
So, there I am, sitting on the lowest,
Most splintered rung of the bleachers,
Talking to him the while.
I might be bubbling down (no straw needed) a 7-Up,
The process punctuated now and then
By a burp of sweet, eye-closing tear-gas.

Did he see the show, or hear the choir? No,
Never cared to. His job was just to tidy up.
Soon's that was done he could get home.
Which was where *I* ought to be. What was I doing
Hanging around here by myself anyway, say?
But I say nothing. A white wad

Goes to his brow, wrinkled and dark-shining. . . .
And then he fades away, gets dim and sepia
And lost. And the page turns to something else,
The dancing, music, speeches, and the plays.

The plays. What didn't we see—remember *Our Town?*
Yes, and *A Midsummer Night's Dream,*
Staged on Midsummer's Day. (And there
May have been—a little late for May Day—a May
Pole Dance, as a curtain-raiser.)
The Hermia, blonde, pretty, and
The Demetrius decided to pair off that summer;
Working together on the play had settled it.
He was the captain of the track team; she—
Nothing special, but interested in Dramatics.
As actors, no great shakes, but with
Nature backing up the magical lines,
They played at least the love scenes perfectly.
(Later they married and moved out of state.)
I wish there were some way to prove, now, that
They went back, the night of the performance,
To the amphitheater; kissed, stifled laughter,
Waiting darkly invisible till the moon rose. . . .
Does soft, silver light dissolve a danger,
And bring them safely through this? Suppose someone out
Of work, and looking for trouble, some thug, came up—
What then? But in the early '50s that
Was unheard of, unthinkable.
Which they knew or rather just assumed. (Half the fun
Was a fine carelessness—wouldn't the play always
End with Titania firmly enthroned again?)

"Small" and "painful": how the two can be felt as one
Thing welded together. He grows taller
And stronger, trying to force apart the tandem;
And one bright morning is graduated.
Every June, Commencement Exercises
For the high-school, weather permitting, were
Held outdoors in the amphitheater.
Ours finally, my class's turn!
We sat there hot and damp in the heavy
Black humanist garb, with those absurd mortarboards
And trembling tassels. Ludicrous; and all the more
If you happened to sport grim, black-rimmed specs
Like those that had devolved on me
During the long assault on Knowledge. And my spoils?
The Valedictory, an address spoken at the end
Of our ceremony. A one-off and no doubt pointless
Performance, which I sweated over weeks
Beforehand, writing, crumpling up, writing. . . .
I must find something that would harmonize
A sense of farewell with aspirations toward the future.
No undertaking for the fainthearted;
But then, the members of my family
Had never appreciably lacked conviction;
Nor was this the first time I had been magnified
Within the hot focal point of audience attention.

No, my first stage appearance came much earlier—
Brief and, to judge by the response,
A flop. Where my teacher got the notion
That an eight-year-old, even with a clear,
True alto, accurate and on pitch, could

Put over two high-toned songs, one religious, one
Patriotic, please tell me. Earnestly performed;
Politely received. That was the interpreter's
Vocation, then, its own reward?
I did think I'd given a good account
Of my songs, myself: let that be *enough.* And yet,
I wouldn't, plausibly, have scorned
Instant acclaim had it been forthcoming.
I took my seat while the applause thinned out
And the next performer sallied up to the mike.
Through puzzlement and flooding eyes
I could see only—green. Leaves and branches
Like flotsam downstream the rushing immense
River of sky. And then, nothing.

Those days, mostly I was the spectator,
Taking it all in. Taking, but also giving:
For the true audiences would work hand in hand
With the performer, their puppet, "pulling for him";
Who must in turn put half, the more vigilant half
Of his mind second-row center—
A benign, inventive form of self-appraisal.
(And a strenuous task. Can there be some
Who *only* want to perform, and never to watch?)
Not that such issues preoccupied me back then;
I simply lived their force, avid to share
In the alchemy, the uncanny teamwork of stagecraft.
Example: that student circus
From a small university in Florida—
That stands out. Those demented and inspiring acts!

Jugglers, tumblers, clowns, daredevil tightrope artists
Who danced on high, to appearances unaware that one
False move meant curtains for the pitiful, broken
Star, flattened and paralyzed on the grass.
No, it was only the fun they felt, or seemed to.
As for the garish costumes, the tinsel, plumage,
And rhinestones—not to let them be transformed
By mental footlights into an orient richness:
It would have been cloddish, a betrayal
Of the all-expansive theatrical spirit.
Go along or not with the enchantment? Ours to choose.
Nearly everybody preferred, as I remember,
To be pleased; banged their palms together and went home
With aerial feats spinning in the brain, magic
Tableaux, and how many zany escapades to dream on—
The lesson borne in indelibly that,
Should a number come a cropper, complete fiasco
Can often be subverted by a skillful clown.

Other thrills: there was that chorus, visiting from—
Outer space, it's tempting to think.
The Wagner Chorale, was it? Anyway,
Two hundred voices' unearthly precision in
Modernized but ravishing renditions
Of Orlando di Lasso, Handel, Bach;
Bliss. And then, art versions of folk tunes, black
And white, both belted out with crack syncopation
And pressurized swells, some dynamite sforzandi
That might have brought the rafters down,
But as it was, settled for five-part lightning bolts

("What You Going To Do When The World's On Fire?")
Flung upward to the firmament among lofty
Cumulus clouds and ramps of golden sun.
For the young, latest convert to harmony, it
Was much as if a wingèd envoy with beetled brows stared
From the recruiting poster, index aimed straight on,
Above the caption: "The Angelic Host Needs You!"
Well, volunteers beat the draft—in block print, I signed.

What else? Oh yes, some traveling entertainers,
A vaudeville, with hoofers and comedians, called
THE FAMOUS . . . somebodies.
I do remember they arranged to have the name
Of the revue, in big, separate, bright
Red letters, put out in front of the stage.
I had come early, to watch them, racing
Around in frantic sweat, set up.
Say there, would I give them a hand?
THE FAMOUS letters—if I would just move
Them, in order, out front. You bet!
But, in the thick of the task, an idea,
A silly one, took possession of me:
To think of myself as the letter "I," and then
Link up with some of the consonants (just
About my height), to see what I could spell.
The result? Telegraphic chips,
Necessarily; but here's a sentence
I remember liking and repeating aloud:
IF   IM   IT   IT   IS   I.
(Ending up a unit again, as it
Had to have been.) "Places," they called,

Waving me to my seat, all further assistance
Snared on the jazzy opening line of the saxophone.

The show itself was "certifiably" funny,
Even though the big-city, for-the-birds
Wisecracks went winging well over my head.
This much was plain: some day I must
Get to the bottom of them. On the spot—
Well lighted within it—plans began to be laid.

Just because it's at the other end of the scale,
I'll bring up here another gathering—
The revival meeting, a regular feature
Of our summers. The one I single out,
Not unusual for the fervor it bred in us
(This was John Wesley country, after all),
Sticks in my mind because of the sincerity,
Youth, and out-of-the-ordinary handsomeness
Of the preacher. "Almost Persuaded," ran the hymn,
But, in truth, we were altogether persuaded, won
Over to guilt and salvation, washed clean
By the blood and weeping our own real tears.
Time has dried them. But not the memory
Of his fiery sermon on the coming apocalypse.
Who didn't recognize the crushing likelihood
Of what he proclaimed? The Time Was At Hand.
Not one of us but had heard Gabriel
Heatter on the radio warm to the subject
Of Korea, the Red Menace, the Domino
Theory. . . . Those veterans listening

Who'd had their combat baptism in the Pacific
Theater paused to reflect on total war, the Atom
Bomb, Asian Fanaticism, Kamikazes,
And Communism. We'd do well to look ahead.
First, lay down stores in the basement—canned goods,
Water, ammunition; but more important still,
Get ready to meet our Maker.
The worry hovering over me always was
My reluctance to greet Millennium.
Must the world *burn* to bring the Kingdom in?
An event all too easy to picture,
Blending, indeed, bleeding into what I
Had already gleaned here and there about the eternal
Brimstone climate of Hell, where the world kept
On horribly ending in never-ending flame.
Sitting there on the grained wood bleachers, hot,
Mosquito-tormented, my eyes transfixed by his
Ardent, sweating face, suddenly I knew
How it would come to pass: His hand would strike,
The night sky turn supernova, sun-white
Beams transfigure all below, as atom after atom
Gave up the fiction of matter, form, the fallen
Rain of vindictive fire tipping earth, houses, trees,
Dominos over into the flowing unspeakable
Flamebows of fission tided to whatever stars
Had escaped the earthly and solar catastrophe: this
Would be the millennium, when the Kingdom came.

So, when the preacher made his pitch, when he
Numbered our errors and omissions, we listened;
Choked back emotion, repented; believed.

That the knowledge could be sustained, renewed,
Become the seed of marked and saving change
Was the illusion. That, for one, the wife—in pain,
Outdone—might at some point lean up on an elbow
To say it wasn't working out, and could they talk?
That the husband who felt trapped in his job, his house,
Might at last try to come to terms, withdraw,
And make a new beginning. That
The child who couldn't get himself across
To those arbitrary figureheads fearfully in charge
Might find a way this time.
No, it never quite sticks. The feeling holds a day,
A week, then becomes a memory, and then—.
By the time the schoolhouse doors swing
Open in the fall, everything's back to normal.

Migrating bird summerbound for the Gulf
And South America, a late autumn passage
Low over the park in midafternoon
Spreads wide the mapped, down-on view of open
Space, brown grass across whose expanse
The tiny figure walks his diagonal,
An everlasting newcomer's minute progress
No moment in your fleet, watch-jewel eye. . . .
Not this, but some unwritten score
Of high and low in the green cabinet
A child takes for his serious playhouse,
Ground bass of pain whelmed over in a free-for-all
Of whisper, hue, scent, savor, grain,
Composed, the slow length of a homeward mile,

My study. November: never a hint of snow,
But downcast leaves, temperatures, cold trek
Through the dark house, bare ruin of a theater
On my way—those signs told that the solstice
Previews, under whose direction, would now begin.
Was winter's gift to simplify, cut back, unravel thread
By thread the tissue of what summer knew?
Openings and closings and openings. . . .
Now perhaps, but could I then condemn the wish to mount up,
Up past the holding patterns and wingborne flight to a stage,
A new year, fruit and flower dancing together
In breezes outside any fixed global compass?
If the boy could stay, and stay dissatisfaction,
Each step not draw him farther on,
Always back to his own small room,
The creaking furniture, lessons,
Chores, his present, and his distant future;
If the cloud ceiling could break, and he be
Gathered in—. But the time isn't at hand.
Stock still, he waves upward, goodby, goodby;
Lets the hand drop; looks around him. And what
Does the player do in an empty theater?
Almost empty. But see, the neighbor dog
Comes sidling up with barks and wags; then stops,
Takes a position; and
Leaves behind a reminder that we are
Earthly clay. On which, to heart's content, dwell
Those who will, those who can.

One blue-and-gold April my older sister was
Crowned Queen of the Beauty Pageant.

74

All over the park early-flowering
Dogwoods hovered against the shaded green background
Like new galaxies in hushed explosion.
My sister wore a ball-gown, the pastel satin
Odd but touching, there, out of doors. She laughed
And sobbed energetically while, with equal energy,
The MC squared his shoulders under a rented
White jacket, coughed into his fist, and thrust
A sheaf of red roses and carnations
Into her arms. Sweet, familial pride
Flooded through me; and, besides, people said
We looked so much alike. . . . So, the Pageant
Concluded, last applause subsiding, all
The friends and relations rose, nodded and greeted
Each other, handshakes and kisses bestowed crisscross
Around, signs of a shared contentment that
One of the community had been recognized
As beautiful, the youthful sovereign of Spring. . . .
These were habits, too, of seasoned husbandry; for,
Since that good held in common never flourishes
Without the single, uncommon effort—
However dreamborne and momentary seeming—
Palms and applause must come down handsomely;
Gifts and promise of every kind be acknowledged,
Take the platform and stand firm under the weighty
Crown, knowing its meaning: that the assembled will
A continuance; that this stage not be the last;
And that the performance move on from strength to strength.

HERB GARDEN

Basil leaves, like poured wax seals;
Hundred-branched candlestick
Of the flowering thyme,
Bee-visited, in a fume
Of gnats. Parsleys, mints, dills;
The green watering can;
Skies, water this side Mystic.

August places its bets:
Ice on blue, fire on green.
Full grown, beyond regret,
The leaves flare and coldly burn—
Spilling five pungent oils
For this bright encaustic,
Deep mint, flashing marine.

SUNRISE
Frederick Seidel

The Academy of American Poets has presented its 1979 Lamont Award to Frederick Seidel for this new collection of his poems. Full of gritty, hard-edged images, yet also breathing notes of tenderness and sorrow, it evokes people as diverse as the Marquis de Sade, Hart Crane, and Robert Kennedy. "Once in a while, very seldom," said Richard Poirier, "there is a book that can remind us of what Lawrence meant when he spoke of 'the deed of life.' *Sunrise* is one of these."

THE PUNISHED LAND
Dennis Silk

"These poems are about a land too beautiful for its inhabitants. So they punished it (or rather her) with a general ill will—Jewish, Christian, Muslim. . . . She's called Palestine because it's her best name. It's not the Palestine of the Fatah, or the Greater Israel of the Irredentists." *The Punished Land* is the first book published in the United States by one of Israel's foremost poets. "The poems of Dennis Silk are better with each reading. Their lines, deceptively tight and dry, open up in the end a world of meaning . . . always rich in recognition"—Mark Van Doren.

LIFE AMONG OTHERS
Daniel Halpern

Having previously explored landscapes both interior and exotic, Daniel Halpern's poetry now finds new voices—"the voices of what I must recall," the voices that "answer back, and in time hold me." These are poems of dreaming and remembering other people. "Daniel Halpern is a young man who has been everywhere, tried everything, let nothing get by. . . . The ultimate and inescapable geography of his poems is the heightened world of the poet's senses"—Stanley Kunitz.

A CALL IN THE MIDST OF THE CROWD
Alfred Corn

Alfred Corn, whose first collection John Ashbery called "a brilliant beginning," opens this second volume with such evocative and formally innovative poems as "Darkening Hotel Room," "The Three Times," and "The Adversary"—agile, reckless investigations of the ambiguities and powers of consciousness. Then the book's second part brings us the title poem, an autobiographical sequence that revolves with the seasons against the monumental background of New York City. Here exquisitely worked poetic sections alternate with firsthand accounts—journalistic, historical, literary—evoking significant moments in the city's history. The resonances set up between past and present add an extra dimension to the poem and contribute to the interplay between the archetypal and the autobiographical, the historical and the personal, the past and the present. "Among Mr. Corn's contemporaries I know of no poet more accomplished"—James Merrill. "Alfred Corn belongs very clearly with the best of the poets . . . who have made first-rate poetry out of the filth, confusion, and steeliness of urban life"—Anthony Hecht. "Alfred Corn's second book goes well beyond fulfilling the authentic promise of his first, *All Roads at Once.* The title poem is an extraordinary and quite inevitable extension of the New York tradition of major visionary poems. . . . Corn achieves an authority and resonance wholly worthy of his precursors. . . . He has had the skill and courage to confront, absorb, and renew our poetic tradition at its most vital. His aesthetic prospects are remarkable, even in this crowded time"—Harold Bloom.

THE RETRIEVAL SYSTEM
Maxine Kumin

The death of a parent, the suicide of a best friend, the growing away of children ... for Maxine Kumin such losses are retrieved in the change of seasons, in the here-and-now of splitting wood, in the features of animals: "It begins with my dog, now dead, who all his long life carried about in his head the brown eyes of my father, keen, loving, accepting, sorrowful." Full of questions that have a passionate resolve, the poems of *The Retrieval System* are not only about retrieving losses but also about surviving them. "We are, each one of us, our own prisoner. We are locked up in our own story." These poems lend each of us the courage to look into our own lives, our own story.

NEW AND SELECTED POEMS
Irving Feldman

"At times Irving Feldman is so good that you start up with the discovery that here is yet another blazing American poet," wrote Calvin Bedient of Irving Feldman's previous volume, *Leaping Clear. New and Selected Poems* confirms that discovery. Here are Feldman's own choices from all his previous books in addition to recent poems that extend—often in surprising ways—the depth and range of his vision.

LIKE WINGS
Philip Schultz

What is remarkable in this first collection of Philip Schultz's poetry is its contemporary American voice; lyrical and elegiac one moment and funny the next, it combines street savvy with the quiet intensity of prayer. Most of all, it is a voice rich in its capacity for wonder and resonant with "the passion & the pain & the mystery of our lives."